J. Milton Bowers

The Dance of Life

J. Milton Bowers

The Dance of Life

ISBN/EAN: 9783337387716

Printed in Europe, USA, Canada, Australia, Japan

Cover: Foto ©Andreas Hilbeck / pixelio.de

More available books at **www.hansebooks.com**

THE

DANCE OF LIFE

AN ANSWER TO THE

"DANCE OF DEATH".

BY

MRS. DR. J. MILTON BOWERS

SAN FRANCISCO
SAN FRANCISCO NEWS COMPANY
1877

To the Lady Dancers of San Francisco:

In your interests, chiefly, and in your defense, have I written this little book, and to your kindly protection, in full confidence, I commit it. Necessarily more a bunch of thorns than of roses, more a broom than a bouquet, you will not, I trust, look for beauty, but for use, as you read: for we need not flowers but weapons, not grace but strength, for war.

I shall not say to you, "Put yourself in my place"; for *mine* is *yours*. If your feelings in reading be what mine were in writing, they will bear me, I know, as one of a multitude, triumphantly along.

With sisterly greeting, but without apology for stepping from your ranks to check the insolence of a Philistine,

I subscribe myself,

ONE OF YOU.

" If in the wanton gesture aught
    Pure innocence defame,
The waltz itself is not in fault,—
    The waltzer is to blame."

" To twine around in mere embrace
    Is but a fancied harm ;
Or arm with arm to interlace
    Gives virtue no alarm."

PREFACE.

ONE of the best, and, when moderately used, most innocent of our social recreations is the dance. And no variety of this, as to either motion or music, is more attractive than the Waltz. This, originating from no frivolous or licentious people, but from the staid and home-loving Germans, was imported about 1815 into England, where it soon won high favor. True, there was a little outcry raised at first against it by the timid or prudish of that conservative island; but it kept the ground it gained, and could not to-day be driven from the mansions of an aristocratic caste, the proudest, and, morally, the purest, perhaps, in the world.

And now is it to become a dream of the past, for which we may soon long in vain? Shall this most natural offspring of youth and joy be swept away, like Hood's Midsummer Fairies, by the ruthless hand of some moral vandal or speculator? Is the temple of the most worshiped and worshipful of the Nine to be forever closed because some sensationalist chooses to label the rite she loves *The Dance of Death?* We think not. We think that all we need do is to expose again the oft-recurring fallacy of decrying what is useful, beautiful, or indispensable, because it is liable to abuse; to show that any of the indispensable

acts of life can afford the base and law-
less an equal opportunity for the display
of their character.

A mere accident led me to answer this
"Dance of Death." About two months
ago, a friend called my attention, while
in a store, to the book. The title struck
me as curious and ominous; and thinking, notwithstanding its fantastic external, that it was some allegory of the
Pilgrim's Progress type, I opened it. It
is quite safe to say of this book what can
be said of few, that from any of its one
hundred and thirty pages you can in-
stantly deduce its character. I read a
few sentences of the preface, and was
still more astonished that the author
pleaded necessity as an excuse for the
publication. Thinking, then, that some
reasons would be found to palliate, at

least, its obscenity, I purchased a copy. Never did any book awake within me such feelings of shame and indignation. Only a strong impulse to vindicate my sex from its slanders (infamous as far we are concerned) could have led me to give it the careful perusal an answer demanded.

And if, in following the author, I am forced to plunge into a Stygian stream of fetid impurity, my readers cannot expect that I shall pass through it wholly without soil. But as the external garments of language, however repulsive, will not sully the whiteness of the soul, I need make little apology to my readers for any forced infringement on the domain of the indelicate. Lest my remarks upon the author himself, however, seem too personal and severe, I would remind my readers that the *antecedents* and *character* of every " revelator " are proper subjects for comment and criticism, especially when we have (as in this case) no means of arriving at any direct and "positive knowledge of the matter whereof he speaks."

These (which, fortunately, we have both voluntarily and involuntarily from himself), must determine to a great extent what weight his assertions should carry. The *style*, too, of a writer, as of a witness, should have much influence on our minds. My remarks upon the author, keeping to the strict letter of the text he furnishes, must be considered in no other light than as argumentative. I have no personal knowledge whatever of him, and if I had any spleen to gratify, I would not condescend to indulge it, only because he had uttered what did not please me. In a word, I would use (as I hope I have) the whip only of logic and of just inference to chastise his audacity.

I cannot foresee in what light the other sex will view an effort that, from its nature, can plead but inferentially their cause. For their sakes I hope they are able, and will soon tell the author of the "Dance," that, respecting them as well as us, he "lies—under a mistake"; but, as to my own sex, if I shall gain (as I doubt not) their approval and sympathy, I shall be amply rewarded for my trouble, how much soever I may be censured, for the sake of *consistency*, by some critics of the pulpit or the press.

CHAPTER I.

The Waltz? the mazy Waltz! be sure
  It shall not be forgot;   .
To us it yields new life and grace,
  Though the vulgar seize them not;
Its rings we'll weave like children true
  Of sun and moon, in our play,
And gain surcease of sorrow and care
  With a glimpse of that joyous day,
When all of the madness and horror and sin
That fools and bigots have bred therein
  From our earth shall have passed away.

                              J. H. CAREY.

HERE are in polemics two kinds of books, each almost equally difficult to answer; the one exhibiting good sense and sound logic, the other, not a particle of either. So always, in some point, *les extremes se*

touchent. The book before me, " The Dance of Death," belongs eminently to the last class, with the addition that its folly is of the most pernicious kind. The face of its pages shows the author to be, in mechanical education, just what he dis-avows—a "professed (professional, I suppose he means) littérateur"; and in true education, or natural development, something very remote from a refined and cultured man. True, he seems sufficiently well-read and acquainted with ancient writing, to treat his subject, however revolting, with some tact and taste; yet he hardly vails with a fig-leaf its nude obscenities. Nor can we accord to him even the poor merit of good intention; for the internal evidence of the book betrays that the author's design was anything but that of " malice " against vice. This is conclusively proved from his own words, in his tenth chapter, as we shall see. The style throughout

has all the licentious polish of the volup-
tuary—all the sanctimonious airs of a
book meant, under the guise of virtue, *to
sap* the morals of society. But, through
all the glamour of the book we are review-
ing, we detect the gloating eye and fever-
ish pulse. If I feel that my mind has
been in high revolt from the pollution of
its pages, my readers can judge how
" much good " it would do to have its
poison cast into the tender, receptive
minds of the young. Let the most blasé
French novelist, not excluding Paul de
Kock, now forever hide his diminished
head. His worst has been outdone by
an American, who, avowedly palled by a
long career of pleasure, would fain have
us believe that his " sense of duty" forces
him to be our "moralist and guide." Even
if the visionary dangers against which he
warns us had any reality, his book is calculated to aggravate them tenfold, by
suggestions that otherwise would never

enter the minds of the pure. If "to the pure all things are pure," to the filthy all things are filthy, and of the last no one can so well point the moral as the author of " The Dance of Death."

Nor need he fear that any one would be so silly as to suppose him a Puritan Minister, and still less to suppose that it is merely from change of *taste* he refuses to continue the draught of the waltz, which he once found so intoxicating. Were this last true, he would surely have told us by what means he experienced this change of heart, and cared no longer to be a virgin-devouring Minotaur. Must we not say of vice as of fame, *Viresque acquirit eundo.* Besides, writing under a *nom-de-plume*, his modesty(?) would not be hurt by any admissions.

We are evidently a very nearsighted community and our olfactory nerves exceedingly defective; for, unlike the author, we are unable to descry the " presence of

corruption" so gross as to deserve the
avalanche of virtuous wrath he sends
upon our devoted heads. Supposing
those who waltz cannot read (and it
would not be surprising that many of
his waltzers cannot) ought he not have
preached from the house-tops for their
benefit? He says he knows that there are
many who can and do dance without an
impure thought, or action, and to those he
does not speak. Why, then, is his introduc-
tory scene laid in an aristocratic mansion?
Why not confess at once that his portrait-
ure of the dance refers to a bagnio, a
hoodlum picnic, a beer cellar, or a low-
class divan? The heads as well as the
heels of those to be found in lordly mansions are, we must presume, cultivated
at least to the extent that no gross license,
such as the author imagines, could be,
for an instant, tolerated. Wealth brings
refinement, and refinement is incompati-
ble with indecency. But this man in

truth describes the manners, and gestures found perhaps (though even this is doubtful) in places devoted to vice, and not those of the inmates or guests of a respectable private dwelling. In the former the grosser passions are rampant, and rule with iron sway.

Our author's descriptions can leave us but little doubt that he "knows whereof he affirms;" but if he had not decency enough to keep the feelings aroused in such dens to himself, he should at least not outrage society by asserting that they are quickened to intensest life in its choicest circles. Much as we delight in the healthful exhilaration of the dance, heaven defend us from the extraordinary exaltation of spirits that the author's waltz produces; from the foul imaginations that any well-bred young woman would shake as a pestilence from her.

But as we fear not the author's bugbears, assured that the internal mirror

will reflect, for our thoughts, only what
we are, let us enter the scene of enchant-
ment, and join the throng of " lewd dancers." Strange as it may seem, the
youth, beauty, and innocence, from which
classic sculptors and mythologists of old
drew their inspiration, invite us to do
so with irresistible allurement. Funny
though, that nothing savoring of a Dio-
nysian revel strikes the senses; no obscene pictures meet, as they should, the
eye; no *Bacchic* music of the cancan or
orchestral improvisations from a Cre-
morne or Mabille Jardin strike, as they
should, the ear; naught but the divine
strains of Strauss, wafting the soul from
earth to Olympus. As I walk into the
room on the arm of the doctor, my husband (who, by the way, does not dance),
a great many acquaintances claim a smile
and a bow. I do dance readers, I am
happy to say, and my card is soon filled.
There are quite a number of small wo-

men, nimble and light of foot, women
who seldom reach to the shoulders of
their partners.   Strange they should
have so many of these ravenous beasts
seeking to devour them with their eye,
to mingle their fiery breath with—well
the artificial flowers in their hair perhaps,
that now and then tickle their noses.
Yes, strange, I say, how many Apollos
like to dance with those small women
who generally need no support from
a partner and are not given to re-
posing on his breast.   One of Strauss'
best is being exquisitely played.   What
may be our feelings and emotions, any
one sensible to heavenly music can tell.
Are the inspirations it gives, of the earth,
earthy, grovelling ?   We forget our partners, our friends, our surroundings, in
these almost sacred circlings, that like
the religious gyrations of the Magi,
permit the soul a temporary escape from
the body to realms above.   This is the

soul-reviving nectar that a moralistic (?) speculator would dash from our lips! We seem floating through ether, far removed from earth and its cares. We are with the gods, yes, but not the sensuous, impure gods of the ancients. We experience not the questionable pleasure of Mahomet's Paradise, still less the gross one of the debauchee, but something altogether blissful and pure. And as its last low tones die off, we mentally exclaim with Richter :

> Away! away!
> Thou speakest to me of things
> I ne'er hath seen nor e'er shall see.

As to exhaustion, why, calisthenics or any other medically-recommended exercise, produces a not unhealthy fatigue.

The description the author gives of the dancing of a couple is ludicrous in the extreme; it utterly transcends all my experience. In the name of common sense, what decent woman would dance with even the most intimate relative or friend in the manner he describes? " Her head upon his shoulder, her face upturned to his, her naked arm around a strange man's neck, her swelling breast heaving tumultuously against his!!" Pshaw! If the real object of this book were the destruction of the waltz, it would be defeated by the utter absurdity of the pictures. That "pure" maiden so vividly described is no pure maiden, but belongs to that class whose motto is, "In all essential particulars, my virtue is at your disposal." A pure maiden does not act like this. She has no impure postures, no indecent *poses*. Purity is everywhere pure, chastity always chaste. Could a woman of the high world, possessed of any refinement, forget herself to this degree? Just think, reader, of the caricature with which you are presented! It was not the "morals," but the *intelligence* of the "printer" that was outraged when our author presented him with such "copy" as "her naked arm around a strange man's neck;" just as if a woman ever waltzed, or *could waltz*, with any one in that style. Let any lady whose height does not exceed five feet eight inches make the experiment with one even two or three inches taller.

But not content with slandering my sex, our author must now slander his own. I am very observant of human nature, yet have never seen the "faint smile of triumph" on the lip of "the late partner,"—a triumph that seems to me as visionary and intangible as the horrors of this "Dance of Death." It puts me in mind of a story I once heard. A poor hungry man stood before a sausage-stall with but six-pence in his pocket, deliberating about the investment of his last cent in the purchase of the huckster's suspicious though savory

compound. He remained so long before the stall without purchasing that
the proprietor grew indignant and demanded six-pence of him on the ground
that he snuffed up fully six-pence worth
of flavor. Upon his very natural re-
fusal to liquidate, the woman in a rage
had him taken before a judge. After
having heard both sides of the story,
the judge asked the poor man for his
six-pence. It was mournfully handed
over. The London Solomon then called
for two plates, and placed the money
between them. Bidding the woman listen attentively, he rung violently for a
little while the money; then handing it
back to its owner, he said, ' Depart now
in peace, my good woman, your claim is
settled; this man has snuffed the odor
of your sausages, and you have heard
the jingle of his money.'

We get on page 28 a picture of a
jealous husband, whom all join in ridi-

culing. Ah! my friends, if he be jealous, he knows why, and that voluptuous woman he calls his wife, knows why, also ; for a waltz is a very little thing to be jealous of. It is really a *be*-cause without a cause. In this case, perhaps the husband thought he had followed long enough the intrigue going on between his wife and her partner in the waltz ; for these are the ones who may lose their senses and give themselves up to a sensual and degrading exaltation. No wonder the husband is " miserable, self-despised, murderous." I do not blame him for scowling and turning green from the snake-bite of jealousy.

If graceful dancing, like that of Bacchus and Ariadne, had always two such excellent results as those given from the "old writer," viz, to make bachelors Benedicts, and to send strayaways home to their wives, I do not see what more our author could desire. But what non-

sense to cite fables about Grecian myths
as arguments!

But what an audacious flight does the
author's imagination take on page 31!
One of the "perfect" lady-waltzers enter-
ing a hired hack to be driven home, very
slowly, by order—in the dark—("down
with the curtains," says our romancist)—
all alone with her newly found Apollo of
the ball-room. Would any parent, relative,
escort or friend tolerate, under any cir-
cumstances, such a breach of etiquette, of
natural propriety? Perhaps he would
have us believe that young ladies go to
private fashionable balls unattended! Ah!
truly, we fear that those gay *blacksmiths*
are seldom trusted with such ductile material as that of young maidens, except
in the fervid imaginations of people like
the author. But should a solitary instance, one out of ten millions, occur
wherein they are, who is to blame?
'The waltz, undoubtedly,' the author

would say! Away with such stupid in-
ferences! As well blame the horses that
pull the carriage. It is not waltzing that
is the crying evil of to-day ; it is the cham-
pagne, the late suppers and the night
exposure after the hot-bath of a theatre,
etc., which ruin the young and bring them
to an early grave. If the author had be-
thought him to assail these evils as em-
phatically as he did the waltz, some real
and solid good might have resulted. I
am far from favoring all the dances of to-
day—some savor too much of vulgarity—
but the objectionable ones, such as the
" Boston Dip," are vetoed in good, if not
in fast society, and will eventually die out
altogether. Declaim against these if you
will, but leave us our delicious, soul-in-
spiring waltz.

The author's tirade is not alone against
the waltz, but the waltzers, calling the
latter of my sex names that I cannot re-
print. What gentleman would descend,

needlessly, to sully his pages with the
epithets Mr. Herman continually uses.
Such language, however, exposes the
man and his motive.   If he have any ill-
wishers, they need no longer yearn for
vengeance, in the subtle words of the
sage : " Oh ! that mine enemy would
write a book ! "   He anticipates this
charge, of course, as he does many others,
pleading the excuse of necessity for thrust-
ing his " putridity under our nostrils."   It
was rank enough, heaven knows, in idea
without intensifying it by word.   But
"his peace of mind" and anxiety "for
what our morals ought to be," demanded
this !   He would be the last to wound
pure and delicate minds by grossness of
idea or expression !   It is, of course, no
cheap clap-trap with him to declare that
he would " prefer his right hand to with-
er than to give offense to one"!!   His book
is circulating now freely, I understand,
just where it will do most harm—just

where, undoubtedly, it will produce meet fruit.   If we sow the wind, what can we reap but the whirlwind!

CHAPTER II.

At every ball
My wife now waltzes and my daughters shall.

Byron.

T THE head of chapter II of the "Dance," we have the following from Petrarch :

" The dance is the spur of lust—a circle of which the devil is the center. Many women that use it have come dishonest home, most indifferent, none better."

The name of the author destroys the argument of this citation. This poet lived in a most licentious age, when a refined or morally educated woman, was the rare exception. In his day there was little cultivation of either heart or brain.

At no time could even French morals compare with the Italian licentiousness and corruption of that day. The people were so susceptible to female charms, that they were forced to examine some of their " prisoners in the dark, lest justice should be perverted by the influence of personal beauty." If France, then, was outdone in profligacy of manners by Italy, Petrarch's assertions, as above, will seem none too strong for the provocation. The truth is their morals were altogether *dccousues.* The undisciplined and ignorant population were sunk in either fanaticism or sensuality, these opposites necessarily creating much social strife and disorder. The fiery women of Italy indulged every passing whim, knew not what soul culture meant, and were strangers to most of those home qualities that women should possess, contenting themselves with mere external attractions that satisfy not the demands of the heart.

Warm, sunny, passionate Italia was the birthplace of the most licentious forms of dancing. Can we wonder that Petrarch wrote in the above strain? But the state of the world to-day (at least of the English-speaking portion) is very different, socially and morally—no less than politically—from that of the Italy of the poet's time. Every succeeding period since, has brought improvements with it, and to-day we can enjoy the pleasures of dancing, as well as many others then grossly abused, in a manner consistent with the most refined and chaste feelings.

This book goes on to say: "The fair women you have somewhat naturally mistaken for prêtresses de la Vagabonde Vénus, are the pure daughters and spotless wives of our best citizens. Their male companions or accomplices, or whatever you choose to call them, are the crême de la crême of all that is re-

spectable and eligible in society."
Heavens! What language and assertions! No wonder that he should dread
the formidable frowns of wealth and
fashion at this audacious and incredible
impeachment. But the noble reformer
quails not, cheered by the hope that
those fair votaries of the waltz who are
not above reproach, will, when they read
this product of a high moral purpose (!)
and a smitten conscience, reform altogether. And indeed few pure-minded
women who have read his book, can now
share in this dance without a blush?
Thoughts and emotions utterly strange
to them must rise up to embarrass and
restrain them. What was hitherto an
innocent diversion, tends to become for
a time at least, a painful ordeal and will
remain so until this book is (as I trust
it soon shall be) forgotten. If emotions,
such as the author ascribes to the waltz,
were at all awakened, it would be be-

tween lovers or friends at least, and not between utter strangers.

The author now quotes some choice morceaux from Byron's "Waltz." This indecent poem might well have been the root, as it has been the food, of the "Dance." The child seems every way like and worthy of such a parent. But as to authors and citations, how admirably our moralist, commencing with Swinburne, chooses his own. *Suum cuique.* For him must have been written:

> "All that nature made thine own,
> Floating in air or pent in stone,
> Will rive the hills and swim the sea,
> And, like thy shadow, follow thee."

What author more suggestive of indecency than Byron!—a man ready to sin upon the least provocation, and whose mind was ever in the whirl of turbid, sensual passions. Is it astonishing that he, or any of his class, misconstrue the exhilaration of the Waltz? Men love darkness whose deeds are *darkness;* therefore Byron would have "the light put out." In more cases than one he has shocked his readers, where the theme afforded less scope for it even than the Waltz.

The author addresses himself to the best people of every country. How foreign to their thoughts must be his ideas! The elegant and refined ·of the old world, at least, will charitably suppose him dazed, should they ever deign to give his Rabelaistic conceits a perusal. But I presume they will be left to the scum of humanity as their fitting food.

How can we draw a parallel between the love of dancing and that of drink? If there were *"anything in"* the former as there is in the latter, would men discontinue it after marriage, as it is asserted they almost invariably do? What man leaves off drink for any length of time after marriage—if the love of it had fastened on him before—however terrible its consequences might be to himself and family? Of dancers we cannot say,—*Celui qui a dansé dansera*, as we do of drunkards,—*Celui qui a bu boira*.

Pope could scarcely have had in view the Waltz "monster" when he wrote:

"But seen too oft, familiar with his face,
We first endure, then pity, then embrace;—

for no familiarity could reconcile us to an Apollo, transformed to a Dragon more pestilential than that of the classic myth. They who understand human nature know how tenacious is vice of its victims, and how despotically it crushes out all the protecting good in our nature. For,

"Our acts our angels are, or good or ill,
The fatal shadows that walk by us still."

To understand fully this, we have but to enter the drunkard's home. No comfort within its walls! No joyous prattle of children there; no fire or food,—

naught but gaunt famine, fear, tears, and whisky; the end—madness or death.

Again, see the consequences of inordinate thirst for gain or power, whereby one becomes a petrifaction, moving no longer in the image of Him who made us. Here will be another almost equally desolate home; gilded misery—naught else. The wife of a Midas or Napoleon may pace her *salons* decked with jewels, but her arms hold no golden sheaves of love; her heart is dead, her life a blank. If she have vice, what wonder that she indulge it!

Take Jealousy—but need we depict this fiend? Who has not seen the fierce gleam of his eye, culminating most frequently in unspeakable horrors.

And how enduring and incurable the vice of gambling! An evil spirit, ever urging on its victim with the glittering prize that allures only to inevitable de-

struction!   The end of all these things
is death.

But who are the presiding deities at
the dancing *fete?*   Those of Hades or
of Olympus? The Furies or the Graces?
Let the appearance of the ball-room, the
smile of pleasure on all faces, and the
quickening of the pulse to the joyous
music of the dance, answer.   We return
to our homes, after a social feast with
refined and cultivated human beings,
refreshed and strengthened, our better
natures, if not more stimulated to good,
certainly not more stimulated to evil.
By joy as by sorrow the heart softens to
a thousand kindly offices for those less
fortunate than we, and the silent trusts
committed to us are generally, from such
influences, more faithfully discharged.
Asked once by a gentleman if I were
any better after waltzing, I replied with
some surprise that I was no worse than
if I had played at croquet.   To vice, as

I have said, belongs *death;* but to the genial Waltz, naught that I can see but *life.*

How can our author reconcile purity of thought with sensuality of thought ? How can a woman be pure and impure at the same time? Yet, this is what he specifically asserts. No shadow of degredation ever flitted over me or my friends, though we have waltzed away many a delightful evening, returning to our homes recruited in spirits, and

> Carrying in our hearts for days
> Peace that hallows rudest ways.

After making some quite inapplicable comparisons between the evils of alcohol and tobacco, and those of the waltz, he proceeds to tell us that it is to "pure and lovely woman" (!!) he addresses himself, to dissuade her from sullying herself any longer with this degrading amusement. *Our* dance, indeed, might well deserve

some of the epithets he gives it, were
we, in its performance, a tenth part as in-
extricably interblended as incongruous
ideas are in *his*.   The female elite of society are not exactly "prostitutes!" argues
this audacious writer, "though the unin-
itiated spectator of their orgies might well
imagine it;" and the soul-destroying waltz
is one of the choice products of those who
lead the world in all that is refined and
desirable, *"perfected by the grace with
which God has gifted them above the vulgar!"*   Those people whom the poet
aptly calls the "glass of fashion and the
mould of form," who could give us again,
in their persons and demeanor, the rules,
if lost, of all æsthetic art—those are they
forsooth, who shock our feelings by their
libidinous poses and movements, while
yet, in their necessarily light and unim-
peding costume (charged to them likewise as a "perfect outrage"), they display
a ravishing grace and "poetry of motion!"

What clashing stuff is all this, to be sure! But what can we expect from the taste of a man who writes of women, fair and chaste enough, according to his descriptions, to attract the angels, as "spitted on the same bodkin" with their "*paramours*" *(?)* in the dance!! Whoever before addressed such language to "lovely and pure women" as is found in this book? Good mothers will consign it to the flames; husbands will hide it from their wives, or thrust it into some corner to be forever forgotten. In no country but this, perhaps, would it have been allowed to see the light of day. Just think, readers, of a *roué*, evidently *blasé* but not *passé*, announcing to the world that pure-minded women listen gladly in the mazes of the waltz to language that elsewhere they would indignantly resent! So, the balls that we attend are orgies! The fashionable parties at the Palace are bacchanalian revels!

The *soirées dansantes* of the upper ten, are the hot-beds whence emanate these orgies,—and we, nearly all of us, are tainted—wife, daughter, sister—because we have dared to waltz! Aye, verily, when this Daniel comes to judgment not one is found spotless—no, not one.

" The social status of these people is not that of the rude peasant, whose lewd pranks are the result of ignorance, but that of the most highly cultivated and refined among us." Were the author addressing these "rude and ignorant peasants," he might have some excuse for his language.   The boor, we are told, could not dance (though he were "to give his soul" for the power) like these beings far his superiors, and yet far his inferiors—if animal desire and brutish passion constitute inferiority—as the author from his premises must concede. Then, better the boor in his clogs, than these "high-strung, patent-leathered individuals," so much more refined and educated; for thus, and only thus, can he dance innocently. We should have thought that the animal propensities of the boor would render him much more fit to create and enjoy the author's "bliss" of the waltz, than would their instincts so fit the true lady or gentleman. But it seems we mistook. Logic is logic, but to what poor sophistry we have sometimes to resort to maintain a crazy idea ! Who can unravel for us this tangle of illogical and incongruous fancies? Can vulgarity, obscenity and absurdity combined, transcend the pictures given us in this "Dance of Death " ?

CHAPTER III.

"Childhood's happy voices
Oh, bid them not be still;
While the heart rejoices
Let its laughter peal."

NTICIPATING in the third chapter the indignation that his paradoxical slanders are calculated to excite, he condescends "to go out of his way to answer" some Sunday objections, made only to be put down. As I belong to neither of the classes into which he divides my sex,—as I am neither an old fogy, quite unacquainted with modern dancing, nor yet, (though perhaps one of the "par-excellence" dancers) an "ogling prude," I do not think it necessary to defend the positions that either of these classes might, or is made by him to take up, although *en passant* I may say that many of their parries to his thrusts (for all the nonchalence with which he treats them) seem to me effectual enough.

Far from being indignant and proclaiming this author a "detractor, a pessimist and hater of all things that are enjoyable," I sincerely pity him, and earnestly recommend him a cooling draught, as also all those of his sex who find themselves unable to participate in the pleasures of the waltz, from a pure sense of duty, or a conscientious regard for their precious morals. Though as to the last, *they* at least could never be lost or injured.

It is evident that our author is or pretends to be acquainted with some vailed and subtle pleasures of the waltz which he is vainly essaying to communicate to

us. Now, if we don't comprehend, why
insist on lifting the veil? Better far to
leave us optimists. How nice are these
old fogies! How good they are to see
" no harm " in so pleasant though dangerous an amusement, to smile benignly
upon their wives and children, as these
enter with all their hearts into the spirit
of the dance! ·What a contrast to the
opposite type, who make a mountain out
of a mole-hill, and who hurl judgment
upon the many for the sins of the few!
Why not leave these fogies in their serene
innocence? Stimulated by the author's
suggestions, they may take a notion to
enter once more the arena of the whirl,
crowd us, the divine dancers, out, and
mar the rites of the Graces with antics
suitable only to Pan or Priapus. In ancient Greece this author would surely
have been mobbed, perhaps torn assun-
der for his outrage upon the taste and
feelings of the young.

As to the "*blushing*(?) rakes and ogling prudes," if they *were* guilty of any improprieties outside his imagination, why should the " divine waltzers " be condemned ? It would be strange indeed if the devil, who is often found in meekest guise moving among the goody— goodies of every class, could be wholly excluded from the ball-room. Get him, O reformer, from beneath, or better still, *out* of the pulpits, before you let loose any more vials of wrath upon our unavoidable short skirts, " our wonderful drapery," and our perfect " concord of movement," (just what it should be) in the immortal and universal worship of the muse, of the " many twinkling feet.'

I see all the eulogistic notices appended to the volume (with three exceptions to which I shall refer hereafter) are signed by gentlemen. Perhaps *they* understand *the secret* of the waltz ; if so, it is not wonderful that they endorse Mr. Herman's views. But it is significant what few women give him an encouraging word. Many of them doubtless, in their sheer simplicity, are still wondering what all the excitement is about. The poor things are incapable of grasping at once the profound idea.

Plato indeed was quite right; for however Utopian may be in some respects the radicalism of his *Commonwealth*, he was not such a fool as to hint even at the destruction of the dance, knowing well that such an attempt would be as chimerical as one to stop the beating of their hearts in young folks, who, by divine appointment, *will* mingle with each other, *will* see and be seen.

The author seems to have skimmed through enough of classical lore to know (what it suited him to conceal) that Plato was not providing against any inevitable evil, in advocating total nudity for dancers. By no means; but he thought that

this delightful, healthful and necessary
recreation for the young, should have no
more restrictions than the competitive
games of the palestra, where youths and
maidens contended with each other without covering. Besides as a philosopher,
he, like Lycurgus, knew that concealment
tends to create morbid and unnaturally
intensified desires, and that full physical
vigor is attainable only through exercise and chastity in the young. But Mr.
H. launches with safety into Platonic
waters, assured that the majority of his
readers will swim them only under *his*
guidance.

Speaking for my sex of every condi-
tion, I affirm that, if there be any well-
kept secret about the waltz, it must be in
the custody of the men, else it would have
leaked out long ago, if the character for
babbling, assigned us by the lords of creation, be just. Can any one imagine that
it is *we who* would turn off the gas? Let

the men try it once, and they will have from us so fierce a rebuke, that they will never again undertake to gauge our wishes by theirs.

According to our author the obscenities of Phallic worship are modernized in the "divine . waltz." Yes, Mr. H., that is just it, and we should like to know from you what is to be done about it? The Pagan worship of animal love is modernized, that is refined, not by the "grotesque abominations" of old times, but by the thousand and one devices of cultured humanity to create what Selkirk sighed for on his desolate island in the words of the poet:

> Society, friendship and love,
>   Divinely bestowed upon man,
> Oh! had I the wings of a dove,
>   How soon would I taste you again!

I am not sorry that our author discreetly abstained here from classifying the dancers of our sex, as he did those of his own. No doubt, had he done so, we would have received as much or less justice than the latter. It is scarcely my province to take up weapons in their defense; all I shall say is, that if I thought I could not obtain a male partner for any dance other than "a magnificent lustful animal" or a "feeble-kneed satyr of dalliance," both brainless, I should flee from the ball-room as from a pest-house, and I think most of my sisters would do likewise.

The ruthless hunters of whom he speaks are to be found everywhere, even worming themselves into the good graces of parents, etc., in the private sanctuary of home, and seeking their game in the public streets as in the crowded ball-room. The "fine animal" of the author is never, as judged by his standard, any better than a fine animal, when taken at his best. No wonder we have to be on our guard against them all, though strange that it is one of them who now peaches

upon his fellows and tears away the veil
for the eyes of womankind.   He should
have remembered that such an *exposé*
would increase the difficulties of the
hunt, however aided by the conventional
liberties of *his* ball-room *commonages*.

But what are you men all about?
Will you all remain listless under these
terrific accusations?   Is it that you think
them beneath your notice, or do you
choose to leave the burden of a reply to
us?   Must we for once reverse the order
of things, and be *your* champion?   For
shame upon you all!   I, for one, shall
never think as well of you as before, if
some of you be not soon "up and at" this
monster.

The language towards the close of his
third chapter may suit orgies enacted I
know not where, under the cover of
, night, and I can only wonder how he
dared to use it.   It is indescribable, except by terms as disgusting as his.   But

what is remarkable, it is "an indecent assault upon common sense," even more than upon society and its festivities.

Waltz we will! . And every woman that possesses a remnant of spirit and courage will now waltz more than ever *en depit* of this "Dance;" so that its author may just as well

——" hold his idle wrath,
While the waltz silvers o'er his gloomy path."

CHAPTER IV.

En "Cœco carpimur igni "!

VIRGIL (slightly altered.)

To write in fitting terms of this fourth chapter, of its audacious and libidinous coloring, and of its still more audacious and false assertions regarding our sex,—against whom the magician now waves his beast-transforming wand,—might tempt any one, in a reply, to violate the canons of good taste. I shall not, however, do so, even though my cheeks burn while I write for my readers the question he now states for discussion, viz: Is woman the conscious or unconscious sharer of her partner's impure thoughts in the Waltz?

This is the substance, the letter I cannot give. The subject, you see, my sisters, shifts, without growing any better, from the motions of our bodies to those of our minds. See what second-sight and morality, combined, can do! But tremble! for all our secrets are out. A metaphysician, whose acumen even Maimonides might envy, has dissected our very souls. Unhappy that we are! The solution of this profound problem is all against us; we are found guilty, and can only admire the acute reasoning by which the discovery was made. It hinges upon an assertion; and what is the assertion?—*Risum teneatis amici?*—Only that any woman, who does not "dance divinely," that is wantonly, is accounted a "scrub" by the "male experts;" and that to do so, she must reciprocate the feelings of her partner. Could Aristotle himself put up a sylogistic circle more perplexing than this? The divine impulse, observe, that

transforms us into full-blown and desirable "experts" comes from the man!
What modesty and self-depreciation, to
be sure!   Was ever before such insolence
put on paper?   Unless we are "experts,"
we shall not be asked by the accomp-
lished roués to dance the "after-supper
Glide!!" What a dreadful penalty! What
a convincing proof that the deep dam-
nation of *consciousness* is in our souls!
But the Rev. W. C. Wilkinson, who
wrote a pamphlet, *The Dance of Modern
Society*, believes the same thing, ergo,
etc; the latter's opinion being based on
the stray conversation of two prigs in a rail-
way car, who would not give a straw to
dance with Mrs. ——, because " you
can't excite any more passion in her than
you can in a stick of wood."   There are
many men, no doubt, who do not care to
make the acquaintance of any woman
who would be likely to keep their be-
havior within the strict bounds of propriety.

We all know about what young men of the "fine animal" stamp would speak after a soirée. One does not gather grapes from brambles, or figs from thistles. Besides, the opinions of Christian clergymen on the practical affairs of life, are often vitiated by the gloominess of their religion. They may be, and generally are very estimable men, but they prefer to find their philosophy by " setting their feet on graves," instead of " hearing what wine and roses say." *The Dance of Modern Society* and *The Dance of Death* seem twins, as far as popgun logic is concerned, if the extract given be a fair sample. I presume they might as well waltz off together.

The author introduces a friend—let the *ideal* "London correspondent" note that he is not merely an acquaintance—in this chapter; but such a friend! One who has gained a knowledge of the waltz from cellar-girls, and has practiced with them tricks which he *dares* to repeat upon *respectable women!* What weight can the mere assertions of a man of this character have? It is my firm belief that no one needs any further initiation into the mysteries of "handling," as little as does our author; and he can sustain but little loss, should his friend break his promise "to show him round" through the dens. But it was most needless to tell us that he was ready to go, if he kept it. The led might be the leader.

On pages 59 and 60, we have something that equals anything in the book for absurdity and obscenity. A great favorite of the ball-room is represented as dancing with a young and beautiful lady in a manner to cause her to fall almost to the ground from excitement; and, upon being questioned how he managed this, to declare that he learned and practiced the method of "handling" in the aforesaid "dance-cellars," among the girls there who were "posted and"—the rest is unquotable. We then get the ludicrous statement that his partner had not a single stain upon her reputation, but she took great interest in Sunday-schools, etc., and was the greatest catch in the matrimonial market; winding up the chapter with an expression in reference to her, that in any country (California, I hope, not, excluded) should forever consign him to the social death of the leper. The contempt with which young women are spoken of, as being, with "judicious handling," the most "plastic material" in the hands of the roué, though flowing apparently from an "exact report," is evidently the author's own as well—the hoof that would tread us down being too manifest everywhere in the glibness of the slang.

The responsibility of the statements and positions taken, is sought to be evaded with some subtlety of literary art. The language is, indeed, vivid and vascular enough to bleed, could we cut it; yet it would yield us naught but the red blood of human passion, and not a drop of the pale ichor of the celestial censor, who, writhing under a sense of duty, makes himself a martyr for our good!

CHAPTER V.

Lives there a woman with soul so dead?
Who ever to strange man hath said,
Read thou my soul for public aid!

Where lives the man who hath not spied
How slander does to lying glide,
And lying to detection?

                              J. H. CAREY.

THE answer to the contents of the fifth chapter of the "Dance of Death" is simply given in the above not very-classical, but true, parody; which means to say, that the said chapter is a fabrication from first to last. This assertion may astonish some of the credulous of the other sex, who have aired their morality in the eulogistic notices appended to the

"Dance." What a broad grin at their expense these persons could see beneath the author's sleeve, if they could get a peep. Few of my sex believe this fabrication, I am certain. How can people be so blind as not to detect the horrors lurking beneath the glittering *moral* veil of this grinning *prophet*, whose book, *nolens volens*, must operate like a pestilence? After reiterating the foul slander of the preceding chapter against us, the women, in particular, and telling his readers to watch, as a proof of his conclusions, the *"contortions"* of body and limb that the *perfectly graceful* dancers exhibit "at their sport," Mr. H. announces that he obtained, on application, from one of the "most eminent and renowned women of America," her opinion on this bugbear of the Waltz.

Now, gentle and ungentle perusers of the "Dance," is there one of you who can swallow the enormity of a great, eminent

and refined woman not only making con-
fessions to *an utter stranger* that put to
the blush even those of Jean Jacques
Rousseau, but "generously offering him
the use of her name" to substantiate
them! Of course, he thankfully availed
himself of the privilege? Not a bit of it.
His greater generosity to his self-sacri-
ficing correspondent would not permit
this. He had to protect from "the fiery
ordeal of criticism" a lady who was herself perfectly indifferent to its effect!
He did not think, perhaps, at the time, of
the "fiery ordeal" to which the absence of
her name would subject his book. We
are thirsting, like Mrs. Sherman, to know
the name of the woman, "renowned and
refined," who "wears her heart upon her
sleeve for daws to peck at." This *ideal*
woman confesses with pale shame that it
was "the physical emotions engendered
by the magnetic contact of strong men,"
of which she was enamored, not of the

Waltz, nor even of the dancers; that she thus "became abnormally developed in her lowest nature"; winding up four pages or so of like repulsive rubbish (all in the *author's style*) by thanking God that she is "married now, with home and children" around her, and so can, with safety,

> " Think of the passion that shook her youth,
> Of its aimless loves and its idle pains,
> And be thankful now for the certain truth
> That only the sweet remains."

Now, after this "round" rejoinder to the experiences of a "sweet girl graduate," we trust that when the author gives again free rein to his imagination (from which Heaven defend us!) he will show a little respect for the common sense of the community, and not let "everything go loose."

If we be not greatly mistaken, the letter, in the extracts, from "a lady well known in social and literary circles in

San Francisco," belongs to the same
category as that we have just criticised.
My opinion is—again from the internal
evidence—that it is another pious fraud,
another evil done that good may come.
But the statement, in the "Letters and
Extracts," that the lady principal of one
of "the chief female seminaries on the
Pacific slope" has begun to read this
"Dance of Death," "chapter and verse"
—a new Bible—to her class, proves, at
all events, if true, how justifiable is the
the author's mountain-moving faith in
American credulity.

What a psychological study, though a
painful one, it would be, to watch the
various effects of the operation as mir-
rored in the faces of the young critics!
What tittering, blushing and amazement
we should see, as the eccentric reader
proceeded! And what debates afterwards, under academic trees, on the
grave and important question whether

the author of the "Dance" really *meant*
it or not; whether he be a saint, a sin-
ner, or merely a quiz! Can such an acad-
emy, unlike the myths in every chapter, have a local existence and a name?
We are inclined to think it may, since we
get five or six lines of nauseating namby-
pambyism in the shape of a letter from
one *Di*-o Lewis (he might as well die if
he wrote it), advising the "dear madam"
(the lady principal of the school) to read
that volume to her young ladies, as it
would "do great good "!!! Were I any-
where but in America, I should undoubtedly treat the whole narrative as a
satirical hoax.

Whatever are we coming to? Several
societies for the protection of animals, of
mosquitos even, but none for those who
are to be the mothers of the coming race!
The city has lately been quite exercised
to hold in check the evils, material and
moral, surging from the heads of the

hydra, hoodlumism, that curse of our new State,—while it not only placidly permits, but approves through pulpit and press, of an evil compared to which the other, in all its forms, is a blessing. For shame, Americans! Vindicate yourselves and your well-deserved character for chivalry and fair dealing towards us, by execrating this "Dance of Death." Whatever may be the Waltz, the book is certainly death to all the interests you should protect. And those who are scattering it through this community, should be at once restrained and punished, as far as our present laws permit.

CHAPTER VI.

"Men who can boast of deeds so foul, and in vice excel,
Are not of woman born, but spawned, of *Hell*."

THAT the author's conclusions respecting the waltz, may not be thought to apply to any period of life, I must state that my girlhood reminiscenses of dancing in general are of the most pleasing character. I see them now, like specks, in the receding horizon of my youth,—specks, shining indeed with the dewy tints of life's morning, but casting no shadow. For in those days there were no perplexing prohibitions from a "Dance of Death" regarding any particular variety in the charming garden of the hop. We

culled from every tree with all the zest
of innocence and youth. We took no
harm, strange to say, till this friendly (?)
serpent opened our eyes by his new
Apocalypse, to the knowledge of the tree
of—not mixed but—pure evil. Alas! if
we were not goddesses before, we cannot
say that his book has made or will make
us so. It would now seem more necessary than before to keep from the ball-
room, young girls under eighteen, who
may not have acquired tone and self-
control to defend themselves against any
impure language of "pressing and squeez-
ing" that may be addressed to them by
elegant experimenters and novices in the
new theory of the " Dance." When
older, they may treat the hand-squeezers
at least—if not *too* fierce—somewhat in
the style Carlyle did the Scotch peasant
who travelled a long way just to see the
world-renowned sage: "Tak a gude look,
my maun," said the old cynic, "tak a

gude look ; it will do me no harm and
you no gude."

We shall have henceforth to interpret
on a new plane the monitory tales of our
childhood about Blue Beard, Red Riding-
hood, and the nursery ditty of the spider
and the fly. We prefer to remain the
" veriest gawk " of the ball-room rather
than be initiated by any of Mr. H's en-
thusiastic friends into the mysteries of
Erebus.

Let him not imagine either that we
can be deceived by the magnificent gey-
sers of indignation in our behalf, which,
at suitable intervals, he spouts up. Too
transparent altogether for us, however
they may mollify or deceive some of our
public sentinels of the pulpit and the
press.

The sixth chapter of this " Dance " is
texted with a quotation from an old
French writer against the absurdity of
some execrable style of dancing adopted

in his day by women of the lowest class, and has of course nothing really to do with the subject in hand. The translation of a single line will show my readers this : "Of what use are all those leaps (saults) which these wenches (*ces filles*) make, sustained under the arms by their partners so that they can leap higher ?" In the first place, we do not make use of *saults*,—that is of jumps, bounds, in our waltz ; the latter is a quiet, respectable turning without any exposure or impropriety whatever. In the second place the words, *ces filles*, show the class of which he writes. These *filles* are the dancers in the low saloons where revels are kept up all night, increasing in excitement to the close. So all this display of antique lore is quite out of place, in the simple region of logic and application. Writers like Vives do not point to us.

Reiterating his "*practical experience and positive knowledge*" of the abomina-

tions of the waltz (which to him we must
presume are real), the author goes on to
say that he is proud that the placard announcing a "Sunday school festival, dancing to commence at nine o'clock," (he
leaves out the A. M.) "does not reflect
the sentiments of the *entire* community."
Of course not! Because a few hundred
bigots, ever rolling their eyes to heaven
in pious horror at what they construe a
desecration of the Sabbath, and who, if
they could, would stop the birds from
singing on a Sunday,—must be counted
out! But just see what percentage of
the moral, conservative, orderly, and yet
picnic-and-dance-loving Germans will be
found to vote with our author. Neither is
it in "the marts of business and avenues
of trade"—spheres always fatal to Utopian
theories and rabid fanaticism—that he
would find advocates for the discontinu-
ance of dancing. Not at all. These
classes have none of the morbid fancies

entertained by reformed, soured, or confirmed " rakes."

The Frankfort authorities, we are next
told, decided, in the interest of good
morals, that children who had not been
confirmed (under thirteen I suppose)
were not to be taught dancing, and that
it was forbidden in the hotels, etc.

Well, what of this ? Does he think
that if there were any argument in this
we could not find plenty of offsets ? Is
not Aristotle at least as good a moralist as the Frankfort people, and he ranks
dancing with poetry, one of the most re-
fining arts ? And did not the strict and
chaste Spartans oblige parents to exercise their children in dancing from the
age of five years. But the book is full
of flimsy paper-balls like this.

Page 78 of the " Dance " is simply
hideous. The gist of it is this, that
those ladies who remain insensible to
what this author calls " palming work,"

or, in other words, those whose native
purity of mind protects them from the
assaults of the " fine animals," are not fit
for marriage, and could not secure a husband's affections ; while, on the other
hand, those who are sensible will be used
up before they "reach the altar !"   And
all this raving of a diseased brain addressed as an advice to us in an inso-
lently familiar and patronizing manner,
calling the "intoxication" of impure
thoughts " *true bliss !!*"

I only wish that the objection made by
the fair dancer to his conclusions, viz :
that no lady will allow herself to be in-
troduced to, or accept as a partner in the
dance, anyone not a gentleman, were generally true in *fact* as well as in theory.
It is much less so unfortunately in this
the New World than in the Old.   But, in
reply to his rejoinder, that an outward
gentleman may be only a "desperate
roué at heart," I have only to say that

any lady will find out that fact long before she can take the least harm from
his conduct, and will act accordingly.

As to the selection of partners, where
it is seldom or never the woman's privilege to ask, it ought always to be hers to
refuse, especially in large and mixed
assemblies, and the sooner that ingenious
device of the ribbon (a foreign importation,
known to few but the Herman family, perhaps) is sent back to its mother country
the better.   If ever there be a necessity
for a directory of obscene literature and
customs, the author undoubtedly should
be both editor and publisher.   He has
" worked up to it," as Walpole said of
the Premiership, and " should have the
place."

In his whirl of paradox and contor-
tion, piling Pelion upon Ossa, to frighten
us from the happy hunting-grounds of
the "fine animals," this author seems,
like his lady of the waltz, to "lose his

senses entirely." It is we, indeed, who should exclaim, " *Speramus meliora ;* one of the best of those better things being the removal from our society, and from all avenues to it, of the "ghastly moral lepers" (if any can be found besides the author) which he asserts it contains. Some solitary rock might be set apart for them on the glacial coast of Alaska ; for the climate of the Sandwich Islands would be evidently quite unsuited to their disease.

CHAPTER VII.

Let the doors be shut upon him,
That he may play the fool
Nowhere but in his own house.

—SHAKESPEARE.

ow many of his sex, I wonder, would the author find to assent to the answer he makes to his lady friend's question at the opening of the seventh chapter of the " Dance." " How is it that so many of you gentlemen are fond of dancing till you are married, and then few of you can be induced to dance any more ? " The answer to this profound problem being none of my business, I ought, perhaps, to let the men fight over it ; still the one

given by Mr. H. is so supremely ridiculous, viz :—" *the privileges of matrimony
relieve the necessity for the dance*"*!* that
I am induced for once, to battle for them.

Young married men may be divided
into two classes; those who are in business and those who are out; those who
have much worldly care and responsibility, and those who have but little. The
latter are of course in the minority—in
many places in a large minority. And
as to these I should be tempted to reply
to this question, pretty much as the philosopher at King Charles' court did to one
equally silly.

The king, wishing to have some sport
with the wise-acres of his courtiers, asked
if any of them could explain how it was
that a fish-bowl with water, weighed as
much without the fish as with them. The
explanations were all highly scientific,
but equally unsatisfactory, till the laugh-
ing king turned to a silent philosopher,

and asked *his* opinion. His reply was: "Is your majesty's statement a fact? Please let me see the bowl in the scales." And so I think on investigation it will be found that young married men of the second class do *not* discontinue dancing. And as to the first class, I presume they would all tell the author that the cares of married life, and the endeavor to meet by greater gains the heavy expense-that our extravagance, but too often, in dress and wants entails, leave them in a frame of mind and body very unsuitable for the ball-room.

The author now manufactures out of a novel called "Gunnar," three and a half pages of most harmless though not innocent fireworks, which he hopes the public will take for solid shot against this satanic fortress, the Waltz. Ragnhild, we are told, was to wed Lars, "*under the pressure of parental authority*;" but she loved Gunnar, and preferred, as would

any true hearted woman, to dance with
him, forgetting in so doing, everything
besides. And because afterwards a knife
gleamed in the hands of Lars, stung with
natural jealousy—and because Miss R.
ran off finally with her lover, leaving a
detested suitor out in the cold, the *whirl
of the dance was to blame !*   Not a word,
" even remotely," about the folly and sin
of intriguing parents forcing their children into hated marriages—a cause of
misery and crime the most fruitful, and
one which our author might have well
selected upon which to blunt his lance,
instead of running his Quixotic tilt
against the waltz. And all this inference,
even if well drawn, not from a fact, but a
fiction ! Were illustrations from real life,
that " blood is upon the skirts " of Terp-
sichore, so lacking that he had to fall back
upon romance ? And could "any man
possessing a grain of common sense,"
think that Lars drew the knife because he

"plainly understood the nature of the performance in which his intended had been engaged?" For what does the author take his readers?

Lead us not into hallucination,
But deliver us from sophistry, O Lord.

Who can blame the "semi-respectable" woman for wishing to escape in the ball-room, the ennui of a grumbling, unamiable husband, in the pigeon holes of whose dull cranium there is naught but jealousy? Of course "she takes him along," thus escaping the misery of her own thoughts, and of his—if he has any. And if the ball-room or the waltz did prove the immediate cause of a divorce from a husband such as the author—a divorce that any Court in the land would grant her—she may well count either a blessing as well as a pleasure.

As to the other totally untrammeled goddess, whose perfections, for some inscrutable reason our author cannot describe, she seems to belong to that branch of the free-love school which is not strong minded, but frivolous. Suppose the dance did not exist in any form, would there be less of those women, who find it much more pleasant "to cleave to all others" and let the husband alone ?

As a rule it will be found, I think, that a man who could choose such a wife ought to be left alone. The dance never spoils a good woman, never weans her from husband and home, though it may sometimes afford an outlet for the follies of a bad one.

CHAPTER VIII.

Illic Priapum pone,
Hippolitum nunquam erit.

—J. H. CAREY.

 N the last chapters of this book under review we have scarcely any thing but a repetition, more emphasized if possible, of the falsehoods and absurdities in the preceding ones. The author would fortify himself with authorities, ancient if not modern, against the dance. And here let me observe that, although he set out by cautioning us, even in a foot-note, not to "*wilfully* construe" his "dancers" in any other sense than *waltzers*—and consequently *dance* in the sense of *waltz*—

he himself *wilfully* quotes and illustrates from màny old writers, who speak in general against *all dancing*, and not merely against the waltz, which, as he says, did not exist in their day. Either he approves of dancing or he does not. If he does, why cite opinions that refer to any and all dancing? Are they given by way of an *a fortiori* argument against the waltz? And if he does not, why is he afraid to say so? Why lead people *ab initio* to suppose, by *the caution* referred to, that he does not disapprove of dancing, but merely of "the round dances."

Is it on the Napoleonic principle of concentrating his force upon a key-position of the enemy's before making a general assault? Does he wait to see what may be the result of the special effort before inflicting a grand cannonade with the same *mephitic* powder? As far as authority is concerned, his cause must be a weak one indeed when he has to draw for support upon the Church of Geneva, three centuries ago, and upon a certain worthy St. Aldegonde of 1577, to whom no doubt

"His haircloth and his bloody whips"

were far better known and more agreeable than

"Shining eyes and smiling lips."

And as to any weighty modern authorities against dancing, I see none in the text of this book, except that of Gail Hamilton, whose words (if not another fabrication), evidently refer to some vulgarities of quite recent introduction, in which, as I said before, no lady would indulge. What "*pose* of the parties" in the true German dance "suggests impurity," we should like to know? And so, by giving a general application to half-quoted passages on special subjects, he hopes to impose authority upon us.

In the very next paragraph he lets out that he refers to something altogether new : "two forward and two backward movements, then sideways with a whirl," has nothing at all to do with the waltz proper, and Mr. H., with his " charming young lady just arrived from abroad," can have of all such fandangoes, as far as we ladies are concerned, a perpetual royalty.

But indeed nearly every paragraph in these last chapters, contains either some false assertion or some squibby and far-fetched analogy against dancing in general. " The young people of the North," according to Claus Magnus " dance among naked sword - blades scattered on the ground," in which, using the author's exegetical specs, we can see the " far deadlier dangers " to which *our* young are exposed ! Following this cue, a city paper, a few days ago, after telling us that two little girls waltzed off the roof of a house in New York to the pavement below, a distance of five and a half stories, and that one was killed, moralizes: "This is not the first little girl who has waltzed herself into eternity"—Specimen bud of the first-fruits of the "Dance."

Again, on page 101 we read: "One of our ablest writers says it is a war on home, on physical health," etc. Why does not the author tell us who this able writer is? We grow more and more suspicious of those anonymous authorities, his imagination being evidently so fervid and even *creative*. And what is "*it*"? We must take the writer's *subject* on trust also from the author's application. All very satisfactory to him, no doubt!

On page 106, Mr. Herman himself, this time playing physiologist, tells us that woman is the greater sufferer, physically, from the baneful effects of the waltz; as what is only "hurtful indulgence" for

a man is fatal excess for a woman! But
where did he learn this? He would find
eminent medical authority adverse to him
on this point. And she is a greater loser
morally also, we are told, because she
loses that, without which her grace and
beauty are but a curse—"man's respect!"
It is amazing, my sisters, how much
arrogance and self-conceit this author,
stuffed with conventional ideas, can man-
age to throw into a paragraph. Even
when not united to moral worth, to
whom, I ask, are woman's grace and
beauty a curse? To herself or to man?
Let history answer. Have not these
·her weapons—like all given by the Su-
preme to his creatures for their defence
and support—ever proved wholly effi-
cient and irresistible? What became of
the work of Confucius, the great moral
reformer, when his enemies brought from
Tibet eighty dancing and singing houries
to counteract, by their wiles and capers,

the influence of his wholesome though
rather ascetic doctrines at the China
Court? He was now forced to flee to
the wilderness. Grace and beauty were
masters of the field to the detriment of
man. It is fated that he shall ever be
the slave of Beauty, be she "blest or
unblest."

> Her dangerous glances
> Make women of men;
> New-born we are melting
> Into nature again.

Man's respect, indeed! We may set
some little value on it, perhaps, when
those "magnificent animals" themselves
become commonly respectable!

In the next paragraph we are told
"her punishment—the *ad valorem* increase, I suppose—is just, her fault being more inexcusable than his!" Another of the million applications of that
chivalrous tale by chivalrous man, of
Adam and the apple! But why is this
so? Hear the reasoning of this casuist:

Because "woman is the natural and ac-
knowledged custodian of morals.   It is
she who fixes the standard of modesty—
she draws the lines limiting the boundary
of masculine approach and of feminine
concession."   "To a certain extent," he
proceeds, "man may *blamelessly (Proh
pudor!)* accept whatever privileges she
is pleased to accord him!"   If I did
not fear to put the author's modesty to
the blush, I would beg of him to be a little
more explicit as to the "*extent.*"   I
would ask him, should his sex be blamed
or not for "striking the iron while it was
hot," the iron being a woman, as he describes, in a state like the fused metal,
"with a pound of passion to a grain of
reason."   It is useless, though, to ask of
this lord-man and his ilk such ques-
tions ; they believe, and always will, that
we were made for them ; that our rights
and pleasure must be always subservient
to theirs.

Could they give no better plea for striking the helpless iron, they could say, "We were 'flown with insolence and wine,'" and that would suffice! Unfortunately for the world and its lords, the very reverse of what the author asserts as to our legislative power is true. Woman fixes scarcely anything with reference even to herself; man takes care or, till very recently, has taken care of all. Emerson, no mean authority, and Mill, too, if not in letter, in tenor, declare that the world will not be better socially or morally till the men get sense enough to allow us to show them "how we would be served."

But since woman has "betrayed her trust," shown her weakness (see page 130), through the devilish enginery of "palming and pressing," used against her by her protector (!) man, he is invited to walk in and regulate matters by suppressing *his own inventions*, or

the vehicle through which they work
best, the Waltz. The wolf is called
upon to "show his strength and re-
deem his honor" (!) by placing the
sheep in some other position more favorable for him. But from these poor
things, as I infer, all law-making power
should be taken! How fair and god-like
all this! What about the multitude of
maidens and matrons who have not
sinned, Mr. H.;—whose "natural aver-
sion for impurity" would leave them
still eligible to serve you in the putting
down of this dreadful evil?

The last sentence of this 107th page,
and the last page in the chapter, out-
herod Herod in their extravagant insolence. He allows his horses — unre-
strained enough before, heaven knows—
now full rein; dashing, of course, his
Bacchic gig to pieces. Hear him: Poor
woman, having shamelessly violated "the
sacred trust that nature and society have

confided to her," the ball-room roués should regard her as something lower than — he would probably have said *themselves*, had he not caught a glimpse of the impossibility.

As to the last page, I dare give only its substance. The ravenous wolves, the "gentlemen, who are no professors of heroic virtues," (not they!) becoming sated with their partners in the dance, dismiss those who are not yet "on the street" with the same easy courtesy they do the courtesans who are! And all this of women who must be (if any are) wholly irreproachable! .

The Indian metempsychosis need have no terrors for our author. If an animal incarnation of his soul after death be either needed or possible, the change can be of little consequence to him. He may indeed find it at first a little strange going on fours instead of twos, but as to strangeness of feeling there can be none.

The spiritual habitat would be altogether familiar. What he would have chiefly to dread from the anger of Brahma would be *total extinction*. Just think, readers, how perfect an animal he must be! Twenty years of toil to reach the pinnacle of filth!

The history of the "get up" of this book would, I suspect, be a curious one.

As to the title, its *cause* may have been as fearfully real as its application has been immorally fanciful. Could the joyous Waltz have suggested it? Ah! more likely that the imminent prospect of a *pas seul in the air*, to carry out the "moral purpose" of a judge, *honest* if implacable, stamped the name vividly on the author's brain.

From many passages of his put cases, it seems to me the author could say of some of his illustrations, "*I know how it is myself*"; for, in many of them we think we see festering the sting of personal

slight or loss.   At all events, what more
natural than that wife or daughter should
seek away from *his* home an atmosphere more suited to her womanly instincts for the beautiful and good than
she could there breathe.   I, at least, ·
could not suppose that the author of such
a book as the " Dance," could fill the
voids in either heart or brain of a good,
refined, or intelligent woman.

Or, again, the foundation may have
been laid by a man of low tastes, habits,
and associations—by some habitué of
dives, beer-cellars, etc., and subsequently
the cesspool may have been a little de-
oderized and built upon by a careful and
cunning hand—by some *cultured* gentleman, who, having the entrée to good
society, descended (for unknown mo-
tives) to pander to the original designer,
by caricaturing its habits—by treating as
deceptive apples of Sodom, fruit fair
enough to have grown in the gardens
of the Blest.

CHAPTER IX.

I utterly abhor, yea, from my soul
Refuse you for my judge; whom yet once more
I hold my most malicious foe, and think not
At all a friend to truth.
—HENRY VIII.

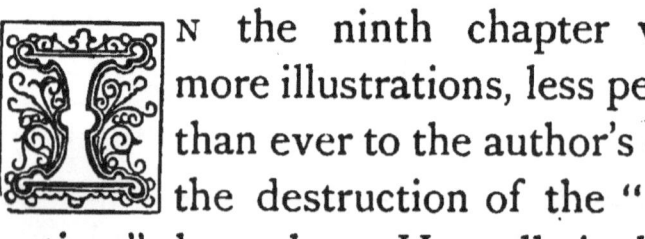 N the ninth chapter we get more illustrations, less pertinent than ever to the author's design, the destruction of the "abomination," the waltz. He calls it the high road to the divorce court; but I am satisfied that could an extended and impartial investigation be made, it would reveal against one divorce a hundred marriages. If it lead anywhere specially, it is to the hymeneal altar, *as stated by his lady friend* at the beginning of the

seventh chapter of the "Dance":.. "you fall in love with us in the ball-room, you court us there, and you marry us there," etc.

This, we think, is rejoinder enough to the divorce-thrust against the dance.

With his put cases of the "poor, dull, stupid Benedick," who, being nothing more *in* the ball-room than *outside* it, (according to the author's own putting), had very naturally to content himself with being a wall-flower,—and of the young and newly-married man, who, having taken a frivolous, good-for-nothing woman to wife, thought to win her heart by imitating her follies, and failed as he deserved,—with such cases, I say my readers will not trouble themselves much, bearing duly in mind his artistic coloring to give vraisemblance to his figures. He appears, however, so sincere for once in his sympathy for the poor "Benedick," abandoned by the wife for some favored one who usurps all her attention, that we suspect some fellow-feeling, in this instance, "has made *him* wondrous kind." Of both these, especially the first, we may say that their own imprudence and not the waltz brought them to grief. Had they not inverted the plain injunction of common sense, no less than of the Talmud which says : "When thou choosest a friend *ascend* a step, but when thou choosest a wife *descend* a step," there would have been little trouble at home. But perhaps it would have been impossible for such poor fellows to follow the advice, being themselves little better than the missing links for which Darwin · is hunting.

The filth of this book is in a great measure its armor. Alive with corruption, *places* cannot be touched. *Mutatis mutandis*, we can say of it in the words of Moore :

You may file, you may polish the book as you will,
But the scent—*not of roses*—will hang 'round it still.

As to the result of Ingoberge's silly experiment being chargeable to the dance, it is too ridiculous, and I think the author ought to treat his readers with a little more courtesy than to suppose them fools. Indeed his selected illustrations throughout are most infelicitous. The idea of a woman's trying, in the feudal times, to win her despot lord from the attractions of the chase by bringing to bear on him the superior ones of " two sisters of surpassing beauty," to essay with him · " the light fantastic," and hoping for any other result than that of divorce or decapitation ! Would the result have been different had the sisters sung or played or conversed or done anything else divinely? Pshaw ! let not our author presume too much on the stupidity of his readers. Once on page 120 the truth emerges a little from the fog in which he endeavors to hide her, when he says: " The waltz may not make such despicable creatures as I have described—(he is speaking of non-dancing and non-jealous husbands, who feel proud of the admiration their wives attract)—but it at least affords them an opportunity to parade their own degradation!!" Well, if that's not rational, 'tis at least original. Why, the qualities that such men possess are virtues, not vices—traits to be envied, not condemned! No doubt, in Mr. H.'s estimation, they would be far more praiseworthy if they showed themselves unsocial, jealous brutes, and dragged their wives in a pet from the ball-room.

The allusion to Herodias' dancing-off, the head of John the Baptist, is of the same drivling, inconsequential type as the rest. Just as if her mother would not have found other means, if needed, of avenging the reproof she received for her licentiousness. This is the way he illustrates that the *waltz* has ever been the cause of violence and bloodshed! And where he cannot point to an *actual* Vendetta of blood, enacted in the ball-room, he will assert that it is "nevertheless declared," and has a spiritual realization—like Paul's Millenium—in "murdered love and bleeding hearts"—an assertion resting merely on *his* judgment, or, rather imagination.

In his tenth chapter ("pray heaven" it be his last) he refers to the latest variety of waltz ; but as no modest woman would either dance it at all, or dance it in a way of which *she herself would be ashamed*, he wastes his wit about the "pleasing family *picture* for later years" that the attitude assumed while dancing it would afford. But if "some maiden" had favored him with such a photograph of her dancing-self, he might surely have risked, like a brave martyr, the wrath of an offended law by using it to illustrate his book, if the "*success of its mission would be thereby assured.*" Besides, if

the majesty of the law could swallow the
beam of the book itself, for the sake of its
pure motive (!), our author could not suppose that the law would choke because of
the motes of a few obscene pictures.

In the following paragraph, however,
we have the astounding declaration that
had he given us such a representation it
" would immediately effect the fulfillment
of a prophecy," that is, in other words, the
" *success of the book's mission.*"   So that
the prophecy and the book's mission being *identical* (as a careful reading of the
two paragraphs will clearly show), to
know what the latter *really* is, or what
Mr. Herman wishes his book to accom-
plish, we have only to find out the former.
This the author himself condenses for us
from a work recently published, called
" Saratoga in Nineteen Hundred."   " In
those times there is to be no more dancing.   The gentlemen are, indeed, to en-
gage the ladies as now, but instead of

taking them on the floor, they will retire with their partners to little private rooms," with which every respectable mansion is to be provided, etc., as this will be "a great improvement" upon the present too public display of feeling. I cannot shock my readers by giving his exact closing words. Surely, after this, it should be needless to enquire any more about the *motive* of the "Dance;" he himself has unintentionally revealed it, viz, to demoralize the world, and usher in a Saturnalia of vice. How was it, Mr. Herman, that after twenty years smoothing and patching to make your pyrite look like a real gem, this huge fissure, by which we can see to its very *core*, escaped your notice? How was it that you could not see the inference which all must draw, viz, that your *pen-pictures* of the vile dance would tend to bring about the new Satanic era with much more rapidity than the sun-pictures ? Ah!

truly, we must say with Confucius: "How can a man (or any other animal) be concealed! How can he be concealèd!"

The chapter winds up with a description, meant to be ironical, of that future generation whose religion shall be dancing. But if we take away the sensual aim and spirit of the transformation (which for our author is nothing more than a Mahomet's paradise), and make one or two trifling changes, we might say that he wrote "better than he knew." He seems to be unaware that the highest expression of religious feeling is in *dancing* and *song*. The first is to solemn action what the second or music is to grave discourse. For, when this feeling passes a certain point of intensity, it breaks naturally into the undying forms of dancing and song. In these, then, is found the highest worship—a fact that both reason and history show. If there be any wildness or

intoxication about them, it is of a very
different kind from that of the "half-
drunk, half-mad Bacchante" of the author's imagination. One of his gross
conceptions—to whom "all goodness is
poison to his stomach"—would not be
likely to understand or value the "true
bliss" of that high ecstasy, so I need not
try to lift its sacred veil. Among the
"whirling congregation" of the coming
time that he mocks, those of his type
can have no place. Hymn-books and
prayer-books shall indeed have disap-
peared, as also the hand-built house,
where they were used; but nothing "un-
clean" shall frolic on the floor of the
new temple, where no mementos of suffering or death shall be seen. No place
there for Mr. Herman's "magnificent
animals," who must pursue their "de-
lectable recreation" elsewhere, perhaps,
with weeping and gnashing of teeth.
The "divine dancers" of that era shall

have no pollution to fear from the
earthly one of this.   Then, as says the
Psalmist, the world's "mourning shall be
turned into dancing, its tears and despair
into "songs of joy."

But it is almost time to stop this needless refutation in detail of a phillipic like
the "Dance," the whole strength of which
lies in its burnished though audacious
obscenity.   We need not concern our-
selves any longer about putting out the
light it has struck.   An *ignis fatuus*
from the foul exhalations of a sensual
mind, it will soon disappear in the darkness that gave it birth; and I should
not have noticed it at all, perhaps, had
I not feared that a universal silence on
our part might have been misconstrued
against us.

No doubt most of my sex thought it
too contemptible for an answer, or they
were perhaps too stunned by the author's
insolence to give expression to their feel-

ings. To them I would now say: sully
not your fingers by taking up this lewd
nightmare, the "Dance of Death;" but
if unfortunately you have already done
so, show that its perusal has not left a
ripple upon your previous repose, or even
a tinge of shame upon your innocence, by
dancing the waltz on all proper occasions
more than ever. Let your acts, my sisters, be the hellebore to restore this mad-
man to reason, even though, like Hor-
ace's applauder in the empty theater, he
may curse you for destroying his pleasing delusions. Drink in the spirit of the
poet, who wrote just for such an occasion
when he said:

> "Ye generous maids, revenge your sex's wrong;
> Let not the mean destroyer e'er approach
> Your sacred charms, now muster all your pride,
> Contempt and scorn, that, shot by beauty's eye,
> Confounds the mighty impudent and smites
> The front unknown to shame; trust not his vows,
> His labored sighs and well-dissembled tears,
> Nor swell the triumph of known perjury."

And while you thus silently but se-
verely rebuke the doctrine of this book,

by doing more than ever what it con-
demns, exercise greater care than before as to whom you admit to your ball-
rooms, and above all use despotically
your right to refuse whom you please as
partners in the dance. Show these lords
of creation that you and you alone are
the arbiters as to *what* and *whom* you
shall permit.

And to the men I would say, as did
the philosopher to his slandered and
complaining friend : 'Act so that no one
will believe the detractor.' You, who
understand what is our due, and whose
external courtesy towards us mirrors
your inward respect and delicacy,—you
can afford to smile at the "corrupting
influence" of the Waltz. You certainly
will not be deterred from dancing it
through any ravings of the author. Nor
will you be likely to frame for us more
restrictions than we choose to use, only
because Mr. H.'s lions are abroad. Let

his fancies devour him, while we, "with
even powers,"

"The rock, the spindle and the shears control,
Of Destiny, and spin our own free hours."

Dancing in general, and the Waltz in
particular, will be, I hope, for you what it
must ever be for us, an amusement *no less
innocent* than delightful.   Remember that
though there may be no actual dancing in
the world to come, one of the wisest poets,
the great Homer, has depicted (after ancient usage) its exalted joys by those he
deemed best and purest in this.   So we
have in his *Dance of the Golden Age* a
high sanction for this amusement of our
Iron Age, as old at least as the sun.
The divine bard sings as follows :

"And here the fair-haired Graces, the wise Hours
Harmonia, Hebe, and sweet Venus' powers,
Danced; and each other, palm to palm did cling,
And with them danced not a deformed thing;—
No forespoke dwarf, nor downward witherling;
But all with wondrous goodly forms were decked,
And moved with beauties of unprized aspect.
Dart-dear Diana, even with Phœbus bred,
Danced likewise there; he touched his lute to them
Sweetly and softly : a most glorious beam
Casting about him—as he danced and played."

CHAPTER X.

" O heaven, that such companions thou'dst unfold;
And put in every honest hand a whip,
To lash the rascals naked through the world."

SHAKSPEARE.

AVING brought this ten-act tragedy-*bouffe* to a close, the author now thinks he ought to respond in a little speech to the epistolary plaudits of the public; the hisses he will print "at some future time," he says; that is, when "the river flows by for the countryman." But we strongly advise his censors not to entrust their weapons to Mr. Herman's keeping, if they would oppose him effectually; for all his promises, he will

take good care to leave them to rust
and oblivion. He tells us, however, that
their chief objection ("for lack of a
better," according to him,) is that his
book "is likely to do more harm than
good to young people, as it will teach
them what they were ignorant of before." In the foregoing pages we have
said the same thing, not lacking *a few
others*, to which we seriously call his
attention. He does not dispose of this
simple but effective argument against
his book; it rather disposes of him.
Still, as he manages to wrap the truth in
a mist of plausible sophistry, let us dis-
sect a little his special pleading. "If,
at the present day," he argues, "the
youth of either sex are ignorant of anything the 'Dance of Death' can teach, it
is not from want of opportunity to be
wiser." Now let me observe that evil
is of two kinds, external and internal.
The first is always real, and independent

of us, as its cause of being is outside us. All external evils are, therefore, proper subjects of advice or warning. Internal evils may be divided into two classes: those that flow inevitably from external evil,—as mental derangements from excessive use of stimulants,—and those that have no material source, but arise from a wrong direction given to the internal motions we call thought. Now, unless the relation between any given act and a specified train of thought be obvious, or, from experience, undeniable, nothing is so well established, practically, as that we should not awaken in the minds of the young, by speech or otherwise, a train of thought which may be pernicious,—above all, in association with a recreation like dancing, so old, so pleasing, so deep-rooted and widespread.

The "beacon" itself, in this instance, is far more to be dreaded, as a destroy-

ing agent, than the latent or imagined
rock from which it would fend us. I
say all this on the supposition that there
is *a rock;* but if there be none, or none
worth speaking about, the office that the
"Dance" professes to perform for us becomes as unnecessary as it is dangerous.
All then is pure loss without compensa-
tion. The author claims that his book
is but for one class (it affects nearly all),
viz: for those who as yet "know no
evil," but may drift upon "the rocks that
beset their course," and so gain "a right
to complain bitterly of those who
should have furnished them with a chart."
Plausible, but deceptive pleading, this!
We all know that vice has, in itself, fas-
cination enough for the young, without
enhancing it with artificial coloring;—
and yet this is what the author has done
all through his book. He has written
of the Waltz in a manner to tempt the
very class for which he professes to

write, the young and innocent, to taste
its forbidden pleasures. Forbidden fruit,
even with instant and severe punishment attached, is now, as of old, the
sweetest for the young. Will they ab-
stain from eating when the penalty is
remote or unappreciable by them? Does
Mr. H. paint the future *pains* of indulg-
ing in the Waltz with the tenth part of
the colors with which he does its immediate *pleasures?* He does not,—as any
one can see who opens his book. So,
then, as this would act only as an incen-
tive to evil-doing, for the only class that
he thinks it should benefit, nothing re-
mains for us but to cast it into the fire.
It has plainly no place in this world,
except as an instrument for Satan, whose
arsenal has been long overstocked. So
much for the argumentative part of his
address to the public.

If those who keep objectionable
works, Mr. Herman, will not neverthe-

less allow your book into their houses,
lest it fall into improper hands, it may
be because they think it, as an in-
centive to vice, "raised by its merit
to a bad eminence" over all others. Or,
perhaps, possessing Rabelais,—whose
"filth," if "inexpressible," is at least
comparatively *harmless*,—and Petronius,
and Apuleius, whose "unnatural beastli-
ness" is not dressed up, like yours, *ad
captandum*, they may think they have
enough of such garbage, and so refuse
yours admittance.

You will not take it seriously to heart,
I hope, that this seeming slight has been
put upon your "Dance." If it was
refused the society of even Balzac's
Contes Dramatiques, with all its "pretty
pictures," you ought to remember that
this was the best involuntary compliment
it could have been paid. The *illustrations* of the "Droll Stories," however
plain and vile, were not half as dangerous

as the "Dance's" pen-pictures. Still, the "moral purpose" of your book ought to have insured it a passport to the best society of its kind! No wonder that you should feel a little piqued that it did not; but unfortunately, as the language and style of your book by no means confirmed its own assertions about its honesty and good intentions, the first (as is usually the case) were believed and the last were not. That half a dozen bad books are kept out of reach of those whom they may harm, is no reason, Mr. Herman, why any more should be added to the lot.

And now, lest it be thought that he stands "entirely alone in his opinions," he proceeds to give us favorable extracts from newspaper reviews and letters concerning the " Dance." As some of these are no doubt genuine, all well framed, and many of them from good sources, and so calculated to mislead the unwary, not acquainted with the tricks usual in such cases, I shall make a few comments on them. Before doing so, I would say that, though the name of the responsible, if not real author, is quite *immaterial to the question*, yet as it was known to many before any letters such as that from Mrs. General Sherman openly revealed it, I confess to being so obtuse as not to understand the *given* grounds of its *formal* concealment, viz., for the sake of "good taste" and "*modesty.*" These may be the true ones; though, having evidently exhausted so much of these precious qualities in the production of the " Dance " itself, it would be natural to suppose that there was little left of them for other exigency. This at least was my stupid view; I fancied and half-fancy still, that *prudence*, much more than any other quality, was responsible for the suppression of the best third of the name. If Mr. Herman met the reception he perhaps dreaded, why, Mr. Ru-

lofson would be, legally, at all events,
quite safe. It seemed merely a literary
" hege," till it was determined which way
blew the wind. But of course I blun-
dered. It was the distress at the "arraign-
ment of his fellow-man " (!) (not even a
crocodile tear for *us*), that made him hide
his face for shame! Poor fellow! The
question at issue having been discussed
by me, and the "good thing" done for the
world, I have thus taken the liberty of
glancing at the author, especially as he
invites us to do so. Enough of him, however. Let me turn now to the "extracts,"
and endeavor to traverse this rather slip-
pery ground without stumbling.

The old breast-work of "no direct
permission," where *names* to letters are
suppressed, is thrown up at the outset.
It will be rated at its true value by the
public. Many of those "extracts" are
undoubtedly *genuine*, if we can use such
a term to articles that have been written

out first by *Mr. H. himself* or his friends and then presented to editors for publication—to office-clerks for *insertion* when necessary, and to individuals for signature. Such eulogies can, as every one knows, be manufactured by the cord, and will deceive none but the most inexperienced. The *style* in five cases out of six will give us all the light needed, as to the origin, like a *star*. In this way, undoubtedly was the scrap of June 17th, from the *Alta*, wrung in on the good-nature of the editors of that paper. The chances are a hundred to one that they had not read a line of the "Dance," when the quoted extract was handed in to them. They are not the men to allow, knowingly, their paper to be used to spread the circulation of a book that would deprave the young and operate as a pestilence in families. Not at all; theirs has always been a clean sheet, and has never, in the most remote way, been the abettor of immorality.

But the *Bulletin* was not so compliant, though we understand no efforts were spared to get its endorsement. The literary Cerberus at its door was too keen and sensitive to have *matter* so offensive foisted on him, or to be sopped to sleep by the "*moral purpose.*" The *Home Newspaper* was similarly bamboozled, I presume, though being a weekly, it would have less excuse than the *Alta.* The *style* and *matter* of the extract from the *Evangel* of June 14th, tells, I think, the tale. But on the supposition that this paper *did* write what is inserted, I beg leave to tell its editor that the *real name* of that "gentleman of high standing," the author, *does furnish* all the "evidence requisite" to prove for the thinking portion of our citizens that the *purpose* of his book was anything but what he pretends. "Integrity of purpose," indeed! Integrity of fiddlesticks! The *Christian Advo-*

cate of same date likewise inserted his
self-praise. It will not be necessary, for
obvious reasons, to draw any conclusions
from what we might read in the *Echo*
or *News Letter.* The last devotes a
lengthy paragraph to a fulsome lauda-
tion of the " Dance " and the author,
speaking of the latter as " eminent " (?)
in "social circles." No doubt; but we
we are not told on which side of zero
lies his *Eminence.* It is laughable how
the paper, or rather the author, tries
to choke us women off from uttering
a word in reply to his slanders, by say-
ing that we *" will doubtless lose our
temper and confess our sin by our indignation !"* This is somewhat like the
trick which many may remember that
an Eastern lecturess played upon her au-
dience lest they "might grow skittish"
and leave her to declaim to empty
benches. We are not aware of having
in the least lost our temper, and as to the

"*gentlemen,*" they will not think that Mr. Herman's "looking-glass" detracts from *their* features a particle. For *them* it has no quicksilver whatever. The *Chronicle* notice amounts to nothing. Three lines, guarded and non-committal. It wisely waits for the *alteram partem*, probably, before unmasking its batteries. The extract from the *Post* of June 16th was written *for*, not *by* that paper.

Now come the anonymous letters; upon two (from ladies) I have commented in a previous chapter.

Two clergymen speak; one a Reverend Father of St. Ignatius College, who, in his commendable zeal to aid what he thinks the cause of morality, plays unconsciously into Mr. Herman's hands, furthering the cause of vice by wishing that all, "*even young ladies*"*!* may read his book. And two other Catholic clergymen are still more emphatic in their admiration for a work the evil of which no one may calculate.   It is astonishing how worthy and well-meaning people can be hood-winked by a cunning business man, spiritually dressed up with care, to play his moral rôle!   None seem so easily deceived as clergymen.

A few lines from each of a dozen or so gentlemen (names given) then follow, but they call for no special comment, being all of a similar character. A lady of "high social standing" in Washington, sends him a line and a half.   As his ladies of "high standing" never have names, we may ignore them altogether.   A Santa Barbara lady, again of the "best," but nameless, writes: "your *choice (!)* yet plain language, leaves no room for misinterpretation," etc.   Can we regard this lady (if not a myth) in any other light than as a sly quiz?   I think not.   Look out, Mr. H.; you cannot draw the hood over our sex as easily as you do over your own.

I shall end this "extract"-review, by making a few remarks upon Mrs. General Sherman's letter (the original of which the *Alta* editors say they saw) published a few days ago. Poor credulous Mrs. Sherman! She received a letter from Father Accolti, and thinks that our hero may be suffering the pains of martyrdom, and hastens to send him comfort and condolence. She soothes the virtuous but too courageous man, hopes he will not be too "cast down," and will not mind what may be said of him—an advice that, before the storm blows over, he may find difficult to follow. *She believes every word he writes, though she would never have imagined the half of what he says to be true !!* Whew! What an admission ! How wonderful is faith! What eyes it can give us ! If this *married lady* needed the lenses of Mr. Herman's vision to see what was invisible without them, can it be true what he asserts—that, with all other opportunities to be wise, " the youth of either sex " do *not need the " Dance of Death" to teach them what they could easily know without it ?* Mrs. Sherman's admission is all the more conclusive on this point, as she neither saw nor meant the inference. She stamps the " Dance" as a revelation (less divine than diabolical, I fear) quite undiscoverable by man's unaided powers, or woman's either. And so it must remain.

We, too, Mrs. Sherman, would be delighted to know the name of that " eminent and renowned " lady-correspondent of your hero, but our just curiosity will never be gratified. There is no fear, kind, credulous Mrs. Sherman, that any " wrong lady " will be " hounded by the newspapers " for the alleged communication to Mr. H.; they know well enough how unassailable is the character of the *real*, that is, *ideal* lady, and will not give your suffering hero a chance to have a laugh at their expense. Be comforted, Mrs. Sherman; no lady, I vouch for it, will be brought to grief.

Before closing these critical remarks, I must not omit to notice the *decided stand* that three papers of this city have nobly taken against the "Dance." In the *Daily Stock Exchange* of August 21st,. is published a thoughtful and eloquent protest, from a lady, against this miserable production of—to quote her words —"a diseased or degraded being." Its blighting influence is rapidly spreading, she declares, and closes by hoping that the private feelings of parents regarding it will soon be publicly expressed, and a stop thus put to its tide of corruption. This lady has my hearty thanks, and most friendly greeting for her out-spoken indignation and warning. As a comment upon her letter, the editor simply remarks that he hopes the police authorities will soon suppress this "nasty book;" which hope, I sincerely trust, he will soon see realized.

The second paper is the *Argonaut*, a critical and literary Weekly of marked ability, that is rapidly winning its way to public favor. How this journal flayed the "Dance," before casting it to the flames, can be seen in the subjoined extract :

"Mr. Rulofson, the photographer, has written, under the *nom de plume* of William Herman, an incomparably indecent work, unfit for the reading of anybody, and calculated to do as much ill as such bold and bad trash can do. Its very nastiness will disarm it to a certain extent. It will be excluded from all decent society. We are sorry to say it is sold by respectable book-sellers, and we are utterly disgusted that it has received the endorsement of certain unthinking newspapers, unreflecting clergymen, and foolish women.

"Immodest words admit of no defense,
For want of decency is want of sense."

After reading the copy presented to us for review, we burned it."

And last in order of time, but not least,

is the withering onslaught in the *Spirit of the Times* of Sept. 8th, by its editor. We feel more secure and proud to know that such a *spirit* exists and asserts itself when necessary, and hope that San Francisco will show that she is not behind this, the true *Spirit of the Times*, by acting upon the editor's indignant call for the stoppage of the further circulation of so deadly a poison. We recommend the perusal of the article to all interested in the protection and welfare of our city.

The good examples of these papers, especially the last, should have stimulated before now, others to speak or act in behalf of public morality.

There appeared last month in a Daily *(not particularly scrupulous)* of this city, the following:

A BAWDY BOOK.

AN ENGLISH OPINION OF THE " DANCE OF DEATH."

A couple of months ago a gentleman of this city mailed a copy of the rather notoriou production called *The Dance of Death*, to a friend in London, a well-known literary man, making the suggestion that a re-publication there might prove profitable. Yesterday the San Franciscan received a letter from his friend in which this agreeable little passage occurs.

"The book has arrived and I have read it. I sincerely trust it may never be my fate to look upon its like again. Do you forget that there is an institution in this country known as 'The Society for the Suppression of Vice?' Why, if we were to publish this filthy book we should be summoned to the Police Court for selling an obscene publication, and we should richly deserve it! Any pure-minded woman would receive a deeper moral blight in reading three of these pages than she possibly could in waltzing every night, all her life long, unless, indeed, she happened to be cursed with a partner in the dance, such as the filthy beast that wrote the book; for to my mind it could not be written by any other than a degraded intellect. Excuse my speaking strongly, but you say it is written by an acquaintance of yours. I am glad he is not among your friends."

Now, I think I can make even a better use for public benefit of this "English opinion " than did " Leone," in the *Stock Exchange.* She, innocent soul, treated it as genuine, and *quoted from it.* True, the sentiments as above are most just and appropriate, but the beauty of the matter, Leone, is, that *they were written by* the *author himself,* or his " right bower,"—business tricks, you know. So that you can have *Rulofson himself* as your Cicerone into the very heart of the Rulofson cavern ; a most *reliable,* if not entertaining or desirable guide ! In this we have again his own *genuine opinion* of what *his book can and will effect,* just as I exposed it in the preceding chapter, regarding the fulfilment of *the prophecy.* " Any pure-minded woman would receive a deeper moral blight in reading three of its pages," etc. Who shall now say that my whip-caption to this chapter if applied to him would be unjust ? Who can afford to shed tears if a little of his leprous hide comes away.

A great many personal remarks upon "this same Wm. Herman," for reasons, my friends, that you can imagine, I have abstained from making. One was that they were *unnecessary*. Still, as I undertook to contribute my mite to nullify the effect of this book of his, some may think I need not have been so squeamish. But they should reflect that it would be wholly abhorrent to me and unbecoming a lady to explore the depths of the cavern from which issued so fetid a child as the "Dance." And to those who, on the contrary, think I have transgressed even in what I have written, I beg to say, in the words of the dramatist:

"Pray, forgive me,
If I have used myself *unmannerly;*
You know I am a woman, lacking wit,
To make a seemly answer to such as *he.*"

Farewell, sweet "Dance of Death," farewell! I have lingered too long in thy upas-shade, and must now move forever away from thy baneful atmosphere into the life-giving sunshine.

FINIS.